Futuristic Crimes of Passion
A Collection of writing by a Collection of People

Intro/Prelude, written by @bluntsbyephresh

I googled the definition of "prose" because I kept saying the word in my head and it felt like something from high school English so I thought it might help. It did.

It was a weird confidence booster but one night while scrolling twitter I read that googling your twitter handle under the google news tab you be able to see if any of your tweets had ever been featured in an article listed online. I wasn't surprised that at least one of my tweets had been featured in an article, but I was surprised by which tweet of mine was used.

Remember when Christmas Eve felt like the longest day of the year? Never getting that back.

Being a conspiracy theorist is so much fun. You're like, up at 2am reading about... I don't know. But a good one. A good conspiracy theory you know. AND YOU CONVINCE YOURSELF. Then you wake up the next morning like "nah, there's no way they sunk the titanic just cuhz three important men who just so happened to be against the new found federal reserve system was in attendance."

There is really no need to mention this but just for whomever's information I have minimal training in this. One creative writing class my first year of college and that's pretty much it.

Honesty is an amazing policy, but I also believe that we live in a society that very often punishes people for their honesty.

I'm a pretty big fan of order, organization. Not an obsessive stan, but a pretty big fan.

Shout out to Seinfeld. The international players television show.

Were only doing this to get our imagination the credit it deserves.

"Bitch, my generation gets traumatized for breakfast."

Between the hours of three and nine am (that's in the morning) is when American magic is accessible to all Americans. Well, everyone on American soil, but more than likely just natural born citizens.

Thank you, Atlanta Georgia for providing some of the most influential music to my life, throughout my life. So basically, the last 25 years of music to come from that area.

What's the virtuous version of lying, cheating and stealing? Is it the same thing but done with virtue?

My favorite kind of pop tart is strawberry, and I don't eat the crusts, so I only eat about 75% pop tart. Come get me America.

I credit a large portion of my applicable knowledge to tv, more specifically cartoons. From school house rock teaching parts of speech to Mr. Peanut Butters ex-wife teaching us about good old-fashioned American politics featuring back door deals and lobbying for privately funded prisons. I'm so smart.

Anyone else out there like... struggle with taking a permanent religious standpoint? Anyone else kind of like research and practice a couple different religious policies for conversational purposes? Just me? It's all about how you "hedge your bets"

There's an eBook out there titled "Marijuana Simpson" and I don't know the author, but that story was mad inspirational to my writing style. So, whomever the original author is. Thank you.

The idea of having followers is amazing but where is the medium between Olsten and Manson? It's probably having roughly 300 followers on twitter.

A Russian guy once said, "I don't need to destroy capitalism because it sows the seeds of its own destruction."

I don't do over positivity. I really don't like deep sea diving. And I only speak with conviction when I'm talking from experience.

So, I recently found out you can fail in directions... that was a big moment in my life.

I like to listen to music and watch tv at the same time. But the music has to overpower the tv, so I'm forced to read the captions. All the while I'm usually writing or typing. Drowning in words. I love that shit. It's how you keep your minds eye at 20/20.

Yea paying bills was and is a shock, and rebuilding credit is tough, but why didn't anyone tell me that being an adult meant outliving people you love?

Somewhere between a short attention span and never wanting to see a good story end, I have never finished a book of my personal choice. I did a lot of 100-page sprints while working a college bookstore.

"The minute God crapped out a third caveman a conspiracy theory was hatched against one of them."

My front-page mantra is "I don't deserve any of this." When I come up, I say it to remember things aren't always this easy for me. When I fall down it's a little self-reminder that adversity is normal, life isn't always personal.

Is there a word for the study of the history of all religion? Yes or no?

"Spent all my cash on a broken dream, went from weed and liquor to the coke n lean."

Being in Las Vegas is my shit. Cig smokers heaven.

Why are people in angry mobs always like ridiculously strong? You're watching a movie and two scenes earlier the neighbors were afraid of the HOA president, but once mob mentality sets in one command and they're man handling people like pirates.

Please, don't anyone feel so entitled to speaking on my behalf that you turn a memorial service for me into some kind of love pissing contest.

I take a large amount of pride in the fact that I have created a world for myself to live, no. No, a world for me to thrive in. Rules, regulations, safe spaces, mythologies. I mean, the solipsism is REAL over here!

Oh yea, before we get too serious here, I'd like to say that I am seeking some form of representation. I'd like to pitch scripts or treatments for a living, but most companies don't listen to independents.

I'm honestly hoping that this form of storytelling brings me the mass respect that I imagine having a college degree brings people.

Did you know that Donald Duck has real life military credentials? Whichever of the wars Disney did major propaganda for earned him some sort of military discharge. Part of his military leaves even add to the plot of the show involving his brother and sons.

It was a very seamless transition from believing in holiday mascots to not doing so, but I didn't learn that not all pilots get picked up until I was like twenty-one years old.

I had a friend; a pretty close friend tells me (as we were in the club partying on NYE) he says something like "I like your brand of positivity. You're always smiling." Which is true. I am always smiling. BUT. I'm always smiling because I like smiling. People like my smile. Women out in public like my smile. Anyway, when he said that I felt like one of THOSE people, ya know, the kind of person who has smiled through a lot of pain. I've been to a lot of painful places in my life. But its always been okay because I have like souvenirs and funny stories and I met people who brought peace to my pain and you're goddamn right I'm always smiling cause if life is all about making the most out of a bad situation then I'm doing amazing on my worst day. Annnnyyyyywwaaaaaay! We were kind of drunk, here's my stories.

Radical feminism defeats Modern Patriarchy
A live reporting of events told by Dr Cornelius Funke

January 20, 2021. United States of America. The cold war between men and women finally became active after a radical feminist group made and attempt on the life of President Trump at his second term inaugural ceremony. Although all surviving members involved in the attack were sentenced to life in prison after long investigations and trials, the attacks didn't stop with just the president either. From the night of the presidential assassination attempt and forward, hundreds possibly thousands of American men holding all different statuses were reportedly attacked by women, excuse me attacked by groups of women. To men holding onto there more primal view of gender roles in our country. CEO's and supervisors, teachers and mentors. Abusers all the same. The message was clear with no end game. Women were no longer going to stand, sit, kneel or lay down for the current role that society has been forcing on them.

By June of 2021 the country was split in multiple aspects of a nation. Due to the large amount of solidarity from feminist in New York, the radical groups conquered the east coast with ease. Congress women Alexandria Ocasio Cortez led the movement to its current state using the social media status and popularity she gained on twitter back in early 2019. She was not directly involved in the inaugural assassination attempt it was heavily implied that she influenced.

Somewhere in the Midwest an entire community is putting together a caravan to the east coast for a large attack on the progressive population that roams the streets of the east coast and tried to kill their president whom they would kill or be killed for. With a lack of gun control each family is armed with enough fire power to stop a couple family lines in their tracks. For a group of people who have been labeled as some of the dumbest Americans, they are amongst the most strategic and tactical Americans. They have learned how to bide their time attack when the moment is clear.

All the radical feminist who layed in waiting for this revolution immediately migrated towards the east coast in hopes to join the movement and fight for the freedoms they felt they deserved. Or at least get a chance to release some pinned-up aggression against any man in their way. Any man that had any kind of control over any number of women young or old packed up dragged them to "middle America". It was a sad sight to see for many American neighborhoods. Some stories hit the news as funny though. The south didn't change one bit. The neutral evil of America if you will. The west coast stood strong as the least migrated area.

The bottom of California to the top of Washington, the west coast moves forward at its normal growth rate, which was already more progressive than the rest of the country. Companies like Apple, Tesla/SpaceX, Amazon group together to hurl the entire west coast further into the forefront of modern technology.

By August, America's surface is at peace due to post Independence Day patriotism, neither party has let their guard down but 4th of July sales, parties, events and cookouts have slowed down most talks of any attacks. I guess this is what civil unrest in a capitalist economy looks like.

September 6, 2021. The entire nation and some others within the extended world stand still while president Trump gives and impromptu speech that aired on all American registered electronic devices made for playback. For many Americans, it is the first time witnessing the full power of American Government. Trump addresses all Americans but more importantly he points a big fat metaphorical finger at the "crazy women attacking good and innocent men" in an attempt to shame the Feminist movement and followers alike. Before he ends his speech, he makes heavy implications towards Congresswoman Ocasio Cortez. Saying, "To the congresswoman from the east coast who has been said to be orchestrating this squad of radicals, this is your only warning." His feed goes black, normally scheduled programming returns and Americans, although they talk about it through the rest of the day, go on with their lives...

The very next morning the congresswoman, her lack of fear and a battalion of women soldiers stood outside the White House gates. Rumor had it that she was going to force a meeting with Trump to present her demands. After an hour of ominous and vague news covered Trump's admin came out and from what we can tell accepted her demand of seeking counsel with the President. Five delegates per party, a sit down that would ignite or defuse a war bomb in on America's home soil. Americans were all glued to their televisions to watch their selected news stations in order to cure the confusion they all suffered from and form an opinion on the events that were unfolding before their collective eyes. We all waited. Still in all our confusion we waited for something to happen. DEAR GOD, IS ANYTHING GONNA HAPPEN?! Then we watched as a helicopter landed in the of back of the White House, the congresswoman and her party were escorted inside and once again we sat in confusion. So much possibility. When it was over, and everyone parted ways and live tv coverage stopped we never thought that exactly one month from this moment a live war would begin on U.S soil.

October 7, 2021: Vice TV leaks the recorded conversation between the congresswoman and the president. The president did a lot of talking as usual, but all anyone heard was the congresswoman's declaration that she would be the next president of the united states and Trump had two options as result of: Step down and comply or go to war. She warned that she had someone in Trump's party who was on her side so a second attempt on his life would prove a lot more successful than the first. Trump told her "find someone to fuck you or go fuck yourself" and the recording stopped, and the live feed ended. Over the next two weeks members of Trump's cabinet went missing or were found dead of various complications including heart attacks and golfing accidents, one of which involving carnivorous goats. We weren't sure who was responsible at this point so most news outlets only partially covered investigations leaving the rest to internet guru's and bloggers. Trump supporters all throughout the Midwest decide they should order an attack on the feminist movement on Trump's behalf as they believe that Trump is way too classy to address these people.

So on October 27, 2021 an entire tristate area put together that caravan, set out for NYC and by the time they made it to the United Nations building, which was being used as HQ for the feminist movement, they had killed over 200 women and LGBT extended members and family members all the same. Over 300 standing soldiers outside the UN building were either wounded or killed as well, making for a very bloody NYC afternoon. Only a fraction of the attackers made it away from the rampage, but the message was clear- middle America was ready to stand their ground for their president. Their current president.

The aftermath of the attack was wide spread depression. Leading up to all this America was no stranger to gun violence but the nature of this attack was so specific with no mystery around it. Just a straight forward retaliation attack. A very transparent declaration of war.

Bloody. Fucking. Halloween! October 31 news vessels everywhere are reporting that Trump was rushed to urgent care after being attacked by a family member while in the confines of the White House. Almost immediately after this, reports came out that Trump's youngest son and newest wife were missing. There was a gasp that could be heard around the world. The scandal was real! The next month zipped past us as we watched in awe and confusion as Congresswoman AOC bullied her way into The Oval Office. We watched as she did all this with the ex-president's wife by her side while the ex-president lay in a coma that the two of them had put him in. There was major backlash and one hell of an aftermath to this battle for power. As the Midwest and parts of the south were cleansed by the new American military, the country seems to slingshot through multiple renaissances because progressive mentalities began taking over the flow of the nation. President Ocasio-Cortez was set to deliver a televised speech on New Year's Day to address the people. There were a lot of questions that required some pretty detailed answers or at least that's how most of us felt on the west coast, and some topics that needed to be lightly talked about by some sort of representative. With the country witnessing changing president's immediately after Trump was put into a coma by his wife shortly after he was attacked during his inauguration. And then after the president was attacked, approximately sixty percent of the male population were on edge due to a rise in feminist-based attacks on men. Two weeks after the ex-president's wife was seen on live television holding hands with the women who declared war on and ultimately destroyed her husband, she was assassinated by a Russian spy who killed himself via cyanide poison in a false tooth capsule during interrogation. A large, unofficially accounted for, amount of suicide and genocide has taken place leaving the population in shambles.

January 1st, 2022. The entire Trump administration, fanbase and constituents alike were all but extinct from U.S soil. President Ocasio Cortez stood at her podium and took in all the glory and appreciation she was receiving from the record-breaking crowd of people that stood in Washington at her inaugural ceremony. She gave an amazing speech regarding terrorism, foreign affairs and rebuilding with new foundations. We on the west coast watched eagerly to learn what our place would be in the new structure of society.

"With the majority of our regions rebuilding and assessing collateral damage it is important that we seek aid from companies located in California, Oregon and Washington. We must rely on their technological prowess to rebuild this nation into the progressive power house that we know it can be." And that was our invitation; to expand, relocate, franchise. Over the next few months many companies took to the Midwest to rebuild America's heartland of resources and industry. Primitive sources of power energy were phased out over time. Many companies ended abroad facilitation and brought jobs back to home soil. Even through the tears of war and devastation, the people united at a much higher success rate than ever recorded. America stood for progression.

With a booming and resourceful economy to tend to, and Americans looking, now more than ever, into the ground floor of entrepreneurship, President Ocasio Cortez offered all tax filing citizens a onetime added tax refund of 20,000 dollars. Not only would this pump all kinds of variables into the economy, it could act as a peace offer for any trauma sustained during the most recent civil war. American wealth rates increased and the poverty playing field was leveled. The result of Futuristic Crimes of Passion.

The Principles of Professional Villainy.

A Treatment written by Marcus Colbert

[play Meek Mill- Pandemonium]

[Narrator] Let me introduce you to The Dean. *show The Dean standing roughly 6 feet and is any man between ages 27 and 31 who dresses like Jeff Goldblum if he only has access to the clothes Johnny Depp wore in Blow. His professional background calls for a short haircut, but his status and reputation has fit him with a very sinister set of facial hair. Follow him as he jumps into the newest luxury car you can think of and speeds down the street. *
He's a slow start boss who took advantage of a few opportunities offered to him during a time of crisis in the United States. You see, during the year or so of civil unrest America went through back in 2020-21 The Dean was hired to "take care of" one of his clients in order to expose and end one of ex-president Trump's paper trails. This act would thoroughly give current President AOC the leverage she needed to make her attacks on his presidency. OKAY! Let me back up a little bit, in 2019 The Dean was CEO of a high-end private security firm. His client list included celebs, politicians and ya know... "Legitimate businessman" ANYWAY!
End music
flashback December 2020 Location: Internal Security Contractors Main Office, Los Angeles County, California
[Suited man] Look, if I take this deal to one of your competitors, they'll take it in a heartbeat. Do you wanna be collateral damage or an unsung hero?
[The Dean] If you take this deal to one of my competitors, they'll figuratively shit their pants when you tell them that they have to go through me. Then they'll literally shit their pants when they see what it's going to take to actually get through me. So how 'bout you take that five and make it ten because after all this goes down, I'm going to retire and you're going to make it a clean break because I don't like being bothered.
[Suited man] TEN?! Do you understand- WHAT! The congresswoman isn't going to like th-
[The Dean] Who are you playing ball for?! I'd take my reply directly to the congress woman since I absolutely love her face, but then how would you skim the top of the budget you were given to buy me huh? Give me eight you take the extra two and tell the congresswoman that after this is all said and done, I want off the map for a couple years.
[Suited man] It will clear after we run the dummy investigation since the incident will take place in our district, we will be able to clear you and your companies name.

you will be well protected during the coming storm. Oh! And as an added thank you feel free to schedule any problem children for duty on the day of. You can plug any leaks before you lead your company into its bright future.
fade to black

October 2026 Present day. Location: "The Organization" K-12 Academy built in Los Angeles County, California and entirely funded by The Dean
[The Dean] So I took the deal. * Sips drink as he looks out office building window which overlooks cityscape* and on January 1st, 2021 ten people were brutally murdered in a hail storm of bullets during a motorcade for a New Year's Day parade in New York. 1 Legitimate business man, one right hand man and-
[Person] Why are you telling me this?!
[The Dean] And eight of my own workers who were either being poached for info or already leaking info.
[Person] Why-
[The Dean] Because it was the first time, I participated in something that would change the world!! A choice made in moral ambiguity...
[Person] I have like, a million things to do. On your behalf. So! *rolls eyes*
[Dean] Do you remember back in 2024 when Elon Musk put together that team of rich bastards and they went around stealing priceless artifacts and then ransoming them back to the owners for human lives?
[Person] Okay, I think so.
[Dean] Well I was watching a tv show from when I was in high school and it really spoke to me *under breath* organized villainy.
[Person] What?
[Dean] I need you to hire 100 men and women 18-35 of varying skills that could translate over to operating a small business with the normal hierarchy.
[Person] I'm leaving.
[Dean] *continues to sip drink as time passes by and the sun goes across the sky*
[Narrator] Candi, The Dean's personal assistant for the last two years was just your favorite girl ever. She's the perfect build from playing that sport that builds young girls into beautifully shaped women, especially when they get a full ride scholarship to a very prestigious university for playing that sport and graduate very high honors with a major in business management, focus in event planning and a knack for marketing campaigns. If she was three years older and The Dean was three years younger. It'd never work.

*Fade to black and open up with The Dean walking up to an ongoing construction site during the middle of the day with lots of work going on. He shuffles through all of the work being done to find a man younger than him sitting in the back of the site. Wearing a red hard hat and business casual attire. He stands out as the obvious person in charge with multiple computer monitors in front of him. He looks up as he takes his glasses off to clean them when he notices the Dean. *

*the two now stand outside of the work site on the street by the Dean's car. *

[Ellen] So what? You wanna rob a bank?! Aren't you supposed to be "The Dean"?! what about your Academy? Your philanthropy?

[Dean] Ugh, it's about status Ellen. You have to understand-

[Ellen] Status?! I'm not gonna listen let alone help you if you don't kick it straight, I got a lot of things I need to do as you can see. I have a whole block of buildings right here that we have to run fiber optics through amongst other things.

[Dean] El, dammit it's too much to explain just to convince you. This is more just me hiring you for a service because I trust your work. Which will be done remotely from a very specific wing of the academy. If you accept the job, we can discuss terms, conditions, and descriptions. Buuuuuut, until then I can't give any more details.

[Ellen] Okay you're being ridiculous now. Look, I gotta go do this week's schedule for my team. After this complex we have an entire school district to virus block and program. I have no choice but to think about this conversation, so you have that... I'm... assuming I shouldn't run this by the Governor within the next week then huh?

[Dean] The Gov- NO! I mean. Not until after I talk to him. And not at all if you decide you don't want in with me. I am not looking forward to talking to him, that's gonna be my hardest sell. And since I know how you are taking your wife and kids, if you want, out to dinner at one of the three restaurants I own and have them send the bill to me.

[Ellen] So, I just say "send it to The Dean"? WAIT!? You own THREE restaurant's and your trying to rob a bank?!

[Dean] YUP! Whomever is in charge will know what to do. And YUP. I told you it was about status. And that's all I'm telling you! UNTIL you make a decision, and only if you make the right decision. HAHA! Now if you'll excuseeeee me! I gotta see a lady about a position tonight. *sucks teeth and winks* *fade to black as The Dean gets in his car and drives away from the site leaving Ellen outside only to shake his head before returning to work. *

Open in random prison hallway, The Dean is being escorted by two guards. You can hear all the pain, suffering, and mental anguish that exudes from the prisoners. All three men stop at a door and the guards let him in and he walks into a secured visiting room and on the other side of a glass wall sits a fairly aged Elon Musk. The Dean sits down and nods the guards leave the room

[Elon Musk] Well if it isn't "The Dean" *laughs* IveBeenexpectingyou! *laughs*
[Dean] That's... impossible. You've really gone crazy.
[Elon Musk] Imcrazy?!Why?!BecauseIunderstandthatthereisnomoneytobemadein Americaduringpeacefultimes?Americaistooarroganttobeashappygoluckyastheywantt obe.
[Dean] What're you- What happened to you? You used to be...
[Elon Musk] *long sigh* Me, Bezos, and the reanimated corpse of Steve Jobs used to pal around back the early 2020's and just fuck random shit up. I mean, the three of us essentially ran the country. A lot of industries were up for grabs after that congress bitch ended Trump's presidency. We had it made when he was in office. *laughs*
[Dean] Oh, I uhh... Go on please.
[Elon Musk] *mockingly* Oh! Go on! I'm The Dean! I'm a philanthroper! I've helped so many people! *yells* I KNOW WHY YOURE HERE! I MADE YOU!
[Guards] *Burst into room* Everything okay in here?!
[Dean] Yes! Leave us the room!
[Guards] *nod and leave*
[Elon Musk] *makes smoking gesture towards the Dean* youhaveone?
[Dean] Ugh, here. Tell me more now.
[Elon Musk] *takes two quick inhales then one long drag* It was Bezos man. He got high on the power he wanted more. He'd do anything to get whatever the rush he got from doing what he did was. And I've only been saying this out loud in mixed company since he died. *scratches head frantically* He was insane. Some of the things I've seen him do. The things he made ME do, still haunts me. Ransoming all those precious artifacts wasn't even the first thing we did! It was just the first one mainstream enough to get picked up by popular online blogsites. We did a lot of practice runs on people who were never cared for after the fact. Then he wanted all those human sacrifices... we wanted to stop him, but we were all in his pockets. He pretty much did whatever he wanted to do up until he died. And even then, he

had the reanimated corpse of Steve Jobs killed and used his connections to get me locked up in here for the rest of my life.
[Dean] How, how did you know-
[Elon Musk] *laughs maniacally and begins banging his head on the glass until blood comes out* CALL MCKENZIE AND TELL HER IM READY TO GO HOME NOW!!
guards come in and rapidly escort The Dean out of the room while orderlies rush in to restrain and sedate him
Fade to black
[Narrator]Whether in prime or after a long fall, I've heard it's never a good idea to meet your hero or role model. The entire experience can leave a person... inspired? Confused? Luckily The Dean was no stranger to translating confusing messages delivered as sentiments and regards.

Open in The Dean's office. He is sitting down when Candi walks in.
[Candi] You got a couple minutes free for me?
[Dean] Why yes, I do, come in. Sit down.
[Candi] Okay. So! They finished construction on the performing arts wing at the learning center. The Organization will be expecting you to do some kind of dedication ceremony this week, the entire staff is excited is to get into the new classrooms and start new course. They're also excited for their pay increases to kick in and you also have until the end of this week to give me your passcode so I can give payroll the greenlight to set it up. Annnnd lastly, *flips through papers on clipboard* I hired 23 workers out of the 100 you asked for and it's been draining. You want me to keep going with this because I'm not even sure there's seventy however many more people out there to be hired. Can you just do the Dean thing and figure it out.
[Dean] Lets push the dedication to next week so I have more time to get in the holiday spirit. Take that back to the event directors at the Org. Also, find some entertainment. Something cool. Like a live band or something. Ya like jazz?
[Candi] Uhh. I guess. *laughs* I'll get the entertainment for you.
[Dean] Ill open payroll after we finish up here so just send them a memo letting them know what it is exactly that they need to do.
[Candi] Sounndsss...Good. And?
[Dean] We've definitely talked about this before. You're asking me to do more for you than you've done for me. I say "Candi! Get me 100 workers no rush." And you come back almost 2 weeks later with 23 workers and ask for a break.
[Candi] I-I'm-

[Dean] No, I'm kidding it's no problem. Look at you. A mess. Let's just hope my brother decides to bring his team onto my staff and then we'll be good. In the meantime, send the new hires through the regular two-week orientation and training so you can lighten your schedule up some... kind of.

[Candi] *shocked* oh... okay. Kind of?

[Dean] You're still gonna have to play main HR and do the meet and greet for them every day before they start their training classes and before they leave for the day. But that's ALL I want you to do this week.

[Candi] Alright... I'm going to go now.

[Dean] Before you go! Get everyone Wingstop for lunch today. Everyone. Just order everything they have and get enough to feed every person on campus at least twice. I'm taking off early. I'm going to see my older brother tomorrow so I wanna get some R and R before I make the sale of a life time.

[Candi] You have and older brother too?! Wow...

[Dean] Stick around a while, get to know me!

[Candi] *Leaves office*

Flash back November 2024

The Dean stands on a stage with his brother, the new governor of Nevada. He takes the podium as the governor sits down next to his family

[Dean] First things first I'd like to say congratulations, bro. Nothing but hard work and upholding your own reputation got you here. All during this campaign did we meet obstacles. Accidents, accusations, FAKE NEWS! Haha. But if you thought this guy was a dedicated campaigner?! Nevada you haven't seen anything yet because in ordinance and cooperation with my brother's campaign I will be constructing a chain of learning centers throughout the state that will be funded by a charity that I am starting out of my own pocket. So, before I finish up here, let me say that it has been an honor working with the amazing people of this state to secure an opportunistic future for themselves and more importantly their children. Thank you all. Have a good night.

Narrator speaks over governors' speech

[Narrator] You see, The Dean has always had visions of powerful positions for his family so when his brother came to him needing funding for his first campaign to be mayor he obliged. At this time The Dean was off the grid after selling his private security firm to one of the government sectors. He wanted no inclusion in the AOC/Trump feuds of 2021. So, he took his new found anonymity and swayed the world in his own way. He donated to schools and charities and took no credit; it wasn't until halfway through his second year as new mayor that his brother took it upon himself to shine some light on the good deeds of The Dean. The two together

cultivated an image that all people loved to see. Natural passion elevated the pair of brothers to the status they hold today.
Fade to black
[Dean] But all the money I've donated, people I've helped along way. It hasn't been fulfilling.
[Gov] Dean. What the Hell are you talking about?
November 26, 2026 Location: Nevada States offices. open Governor's office, Dean sits on one side and the governor sits on the other. Governors secretary sits across the room
[Dean] I..I'm not sure. Look I need to talk to you.
[Gov] Yes! Duh! That's why you're here. Stop playing!
[Dean] *lights cigar* D'you mind if I smoke?! I'm gonna smoke!
[Gov] If you don't believe the lie, you're about to tell by now you shouldn't have come to see me today, now get on with it.
[Dean] *points to secretary* She gotta be in here? She's lovely but she gotta go. Can't do it with her here.
[Gov] Audrey, can you? *Nods at door*
[Audrey] *leaves*
[Dean] I'm going to rob the Great Bank of Nevada and I need you to not stop me, convince our little brother to help me and also get my heist team for me. *puffs cigar smugly*
[Gov] You're a fucking joke.
[Dean] *exhales smoke* I'm a fucking visionary. Ellen has already shown slight interest; he at least wants to know how I think I'm gonna pull this off. And I don't need you to NOT stop me, I just need you to potentially downplay any questions that I may have something to do with *stands and flourishes hands* THE DEAN OF CRIME! *sits down* so yea. I pretty much just need you to send me a group of bank robbing murderers. Henchmen if you will. Can't have em on my payroll though. Too dirty.
[Gov] Coming from you, Ellen being slightly interested doesn't mean shit, and you know that. What is The Dean of Crime?! Look Dean I'm trying my best to take you seriously, but this is a hard sale.
[Dean] I want to usher in an era of modern organized crime. Ranks, politics, rules of engagement. I've spent enough time hedging old bets and clearing my conscience. 2016-2020 we had Trump's rise and fall and all the villains that came out during that time. I personally helped with his downfall... It's been a long road for both of us but things I did. ME! Those actions put us BOTH in the positions we're in.

[Gov] What do you mean you-?! Hold up. Let me remind you before you martyr yourself, we all lived good lives with our day jobs. You had to go into hiding because you saw opportunity in a coming war, and you ruined your brand for money! I came to you with a smart campaign that would simultaneously put me in office and give your reputation the public renewal that it so desperately needed.

[Dean] I have a vision. *stands up and goes over to look out nearest window* And I'm GOING to see it through. You said at my college graduation party that you've never seen someone with the ability to see his vision through and through like you have growing up with me. We both know you didn't just say that because it sounded good. Now, I'd like for my brothers to fall in some kind of line with me. I can offer positions of power that even look appealing to someone who already has so much power... but if you choose to oppose it'll just have to be good old arch enemy story.

begin playing "stick talk-future

[Gov] Here *writes on paper, gives to The Dean* text that number. Wait for the reply. Then tell them what you need. Now please. Leave my office. I've had a long day.

[Dean] *snatches paper* okay. Thanks, I'm gonna. Go now.

[Gov] If this vision of yours is seen through. I want whatever top spot you have. Good luck brother.

fade to black.

[Narrator] You know what they say: unlucky at cards lucky at a whole bunch of other shit. Hard sale but The Dean closed the deal. Maybe it was the passion in his speech, maybe it was the day worn mind of his brother governor. But it was more than likely due to the fact that The Dean knew how to bide his time and play every. Last. Card he was dealt. Let's see what he does with his next hand.

end music. open prison hallway, two guards walk towards door at the end

[Guard1] They say he's been losing it all day about some kind of premonition. I think he finally went off the deep end. If there's an end deeper than where he's at right now.

[Guard2] Ya never know. I heard Bezos put some kind of sixth sense app chip in his brain back in the day. A couple day shift guards say he was talking about a "kingdom of kids" months before that town in the Midwest was taken over by teenagers.

[One] Oh don't tell me you buy into that shit?! Teens and preteens have had control of Chicago since 2012, anyone could have called that, learn your rap history. Its important. *opens door to reveal an insane shouting Elon Musk behind the glass wall*

[Elon Musk] *laughs* He's gonna do it! Final green light and now it's on! *English accent* I do pray thee guvnor can yeh spot a cuppa FUCKING MURDERERS! *laughs*

[One] See what I mean? He's fucking crazy.

[Elon Musk] *Whispers* The Dean of Crime is coming to control the population!

[Two] Yea. Yea. I never said I understand him. I was jus- WAIT! What's he holding?! We got a sharp object! Call it in!

[Elon Musk] *stabs self in chest three times* the children are the future.

[One] I think he's...

[Two] Mackenzie isn't gonna like this.

[Woman's voice OS] That's Warden to you! And if you wanna keep your job I suggest you clock out and leave before you have to file any reports on this!

The Dean and Candi sit in his office for their weekly meeting. Candi sips coffee while The Dean has cognac and a cigar

[Candi] You do realize it 10:23 AM right?! And you're drinking and smoking. Okay so you're aware of that.

[Dean] Well its two days before Christmas and I got this dedication to speak at tomorrow soooo. I'm being generous with life.

[Candi] With. Lif-okay. I've started workshopping a schedule for next year and I-

[Dean] OH! That reminds me! I have something for you. *gives her envelope off his desk*

[Candi] *opens and reads card* There's a check. For 25,000 dollars. And the card says Candi15 and a line of random numbers and letters? What's this?

[Dean] Its your Christmas present. More specifically. Your signing bonus and new employee credentials. I'm promoting you. To Head Program Director.

[Candi] Promo- What do you-? But that's your job. I can't.

[Dean] I know you weren't shooting for my spot within the first two years of being my assistant. I know you don't feel properly or formally trained, but I'm leaving again. I'm on my way to cultivating a new image for myself. You'll start January fifteenth and I'm going to announce it tomorrow during my speech.

[Candi] But. Sir. I've always enjoyed working for you. Everything you've done for the children of this rebirthed nation is a constant inspiration to me. I Lov...

[Dean] If you're inspired by my work then we have a shared vision for the future of these children and if that is the case then The Organization is still in good hands. Candi You're going to do amazing. Merry Christmas and Happy New Year.

fast forward over the sunset cityscape to later that night. The Dean checks his cellphone to see a missed call and a voicemail. Classic Ellen

[Ellen] *Leaving voice message* Dean! Its Ellen. Obviously. Uhh. I just got off the phone with The Governor. Give me a call back and lets setup a game plan for this job you need done. I'm assuming you'd wanna do it sooner rather than later. Anyway. Just call me back.

[Narrator] It's all about the game you play, well that's what The Dean always says. As all of the pieces fall into very specific places The Dean quietly but effectively falls out of the public eye and begins planning his first heist.

February 2027. Location: The Dean's remote home office
Text messages between then Dean and squad leader weapons expert
Dean: Need job done. Gov sent me.
SLWE: Group 7 package includes:
Four front line armed guards
Two drivers
Weapons will be provided; cost of ammo and any other explosives will be added to bill.
Civilian casualty extra 2,000 dollars per body
Crew Casualty 50,000 dollars life insurance policy
Standby to be scheduled for meeting with team before date of heist.
I must warn you now once you're meeting is scheduled it cannot be changed, rescheduled or postponed. Missing the meeting will result in being blacklisted in our system as unavailable for business.
Dean: Oh, Okay. That sounds perfect, I guess.
SL: This is an automated response system. Your scheduled meeting day is for Sunday May 23, 2027. Please reply to this message with the address for the location in which you'd like to have your meeting take place. Agents will respond to the location at exactly 3PM. A successful meeting guarantees a successful heist. Thank you for your business, our motto is making sure your heist plan is saw through. This message thread will automatically delete in one hour.

The Dean replies with his home office address and deletes the message. Fade to black

April 20, 2027. Orange County, California. Open The Dean at the front door of a modern looking house with a tinted glass front wall instead of normal...house parts. He walks up and goes to immediately knock on the door before noticing a doorbell touchpad on the glass. He presses it and cell phone chime can be faintly heard before the doors pops open and The Dean lets himself in where he is met by Ellen

[Ellen] Come to my office we can talk in there. The kids are all having playdates here and Lauryn is hosting some kind of Virtual Sip and paint. I mean I made the program for her, but I don't get it ya know? Anyway. There's drunk bitches and toddlers stumbling around so let's go in my office.

[Dean] Oh. How lovely. I mean you have like six bedrooms, two living rooms, a den and a playroom but yea. Let's go in your office. Lemme get a map of this place before I leave so I can find my way to that book club and see if anyone in there is worth buying a cab for tomorrow morning.

[Ellen] Yea yea shut the fuck up those orange county moms would chew you up and spit you out. *Closes door* so what's up? I'm assuming you got my voicemail. Tell me about The Dean of Crime and how people aren't going to make a connection to you the guy whose name is Dean and is widely referred to as "The Dean"

[Dean] Okay. First of all. I'm not gonna talk to you without a cigarette and a drink, but I know you got a family, so I'll settle for a cigar and drink. *sits down in a chair at a table* ooh! This is comfortable! How much this cost?

[Ellen] *Pours two drinks* The humidor is the silver door at the bottom over there. Take your pick. I just got the Bennett Family brand there really pure. Money, money, money. They were a gift from a client I don't know how much they cost Dean.

[Dean] *Takes Cigar and sniffs it* cigarettes on cigarettes my momma think I STANK! *Lights cigar* *Sips drink* No but you've looked it up I'm sure. All that tech you use you could scan it or something and it'll tell you everything going back to whose idea it was to start the company that makes this chair.

[Ellen] Dean will you focus! I don't have all day.

[Dean] Alright. I'm going to just give a full-blown run down. Keep up as best you can and save all questions until the end. Okay? Okay. *inhales smoke* The day after I talked to you, I went to Washington State Prison to see popular prisoner Elon Musk. Who by the way is bat shit crazy, so I go see him and like I said he's lost it in there. I mean. He was always a little off even before "The Merger" but in that cell. It was just. Scary. After being escorted out by security because Elon uh... had a breakdown. I was sent to speak with the warden, who just so happens to be the one McKenzie Tutle Bezos. Billionaire lady Bezos has been in control of the American prison system since Bezos died. Ya know, you say the OC moms would chew me up, but this old San Francisco mom laid some hot pillow talk on me. Told me how Jeff messed with the wires in Elon's brain and drove him crazy before pinning all their crimes on him when he found out Elon and McKenzie became close after Jeff and McKenzie divorced. At the time Jeff had too much power and the best she could do for Elon was get him placed in her main yard so at least she could get him the health care he so desperately needed. And If holding a straight face through that conversation didn't almost give me an aneurism the next sequence of sentences out of her mouth really blew my mind. She told me that roughly six months into Elon being admitted into her system he made one specific request that always stood out to her. He requested that she give me an envelope if and only if I came to visit him...It Said on the front, "Dean Ables" I never use my whole name. but I had to use it to get into the gates and the visiting area and what not...

[Ellen] well?! What was in it?!

[Dean] Didn't I say hold all questions until the end? The envelope was pretty uneventful honestly. Some old tesla concept blueprints, a little money looked to be stuffed in there in a panic, and a couple of top-secret documents about SpaceX that aren't so top secret anymore.

[Ellen] Oh, that is-

[Dean] UNTIL! I noticed inside the envelope there was some kind of code in big red letters! I figured maybe it was just some kind of manufactures code until I googled it. Are you familiar with the sequence "XLRCV22"?

[Ellen] Not really.

[Dean] NEITHER WAS GOOGLE! Or... any of the other sites. BUT when I searched it on the amazon online store it led to a link that had like ten more links within it and the final link led to an old pdf file downloadable on the even older SpaceX website. So, I downloaded it onto this *Puts usb drive on the table* Any questions from the crowd?

[Ellen] So, Elon Musk left a bunch of old ass information to you. And you don't know what it's good for. Why did you go see Elon Musk anyway? *Puts drive into computer and begins looking through files* so you're just gonna ignore me? Sit there and smoke an expensive cigar in an expensive chair and ig- oh... OH! OH MY! Do you? Do you know what this is on here?! Its-

[Dean] Yes. Physical and virtual security system blueprints for the Las Vegas State Bank. And I don't know if that's the bank that holds all current and future access codes to the Money Transfer Network of Vegas or not, but *shrugs* I also don't know if the location for the safety deposit box that holds all of them is included in the given schematics of the bank or not. But feel free to ya know, check!

[Ellen] *focused on screen* Are you telling me that Elon Musk somehow knew- knew what exactly?! What do we even do with this information?! I'm so!

[Dean] Yea I felt the same way as you for a good five minutes. And its beeeeeen *checks watch* six minutes for you. So that means I'm in charge. C'mon let's go for a drive I'll tell you more about it on the way.

*The Dean and Ellen leave and get into The Dean's triple black 1987 Monte Carlo SS and drive off as we see the entire cityscape of the beautiful Orange County. Rise into the sky as the Sun sets and night shift starts. Grand Theft Auto V Style pan around to find The Dean, alone now, valet parking his car outside a very expensive restaurant in Los Angeles County he rushes in and finds a dark-haired woman and sits in front of her, camera angle focuses on only The Dean hide the reveal for dark-haired woman *
Play Consideration- Rihanna Ft SZA

[Woman] You know if you weren't such a lovely person, I'd be pretty pissed that you're late every time we meet. Especially because you always call me first. So, remember that. Now, what do you want love?

[Dean] I wouldn't love you so much if you weren't always just a lil pissed off at me. You know why I'm here. I'm finally gonna do the thing we talked about that after we saved all those kids from the Fox News work camp back in 2025... The plan is a little different, but I still need you. Are you ready to come back to me?

Pan camera around to reveal Rihanna looking exactly like she did in 2018 event though the year is currently 2027

[2018 Rihanna] Awe Dean that's so sweet you really believe in a better future for the children. We did work really well together I can't lie you're just so amazing I don't know what it is about you. But you're also really dangerous Dean. I mean, I don't think you're a murderer or anything I'm in love with you but when you think someone deserves to die you kill them. That scares me sometimes.

[Dean] C'mon Rih, don't you want to be part of something bigger than anything you've ever done before and that's saying a lot of for someone who empowered genders, sexualities, and creatives all alike. Constant diplomacy within your home nation, high political value. I mean you and I together saved over 100 young children when we raided that work camp. I only killed security guards who were tormenting young children. And technically, I didn't kill all those people, the government did, so. *sips drink* nothing to be scared of.

[2018 Rihanna] I'm not gonna lie you always know how to pique my interest Dean, that's why I always answer when you call you smooth son of a bitch. I'm yours. Now let's go back to your place so you can tell me all about your little plan to control the population and reassure the future. *Smiles and sips drink*

fade to black

May 23, 2027 Location: The Dean's secret home office. In a rather large, completely closed off room stand The Dean, The Gov, Ellen, Rihanna circa 2018, a man dressed in military fatigues whom we assume to be the Squad Leader Weapons Expert and 3 men 3 women who all oddly look weirdly alike, The drivers and shooters

[SLWE] *To The Dean in a southern accent that's also been to 5 years of college* Nice to meet you son my name is General Stan Gibbs! I am your Squad Leader Weapons Expert but from here on out you can refer to me solely as General, although this will be the only conversation we have because any government inclusion in this heist is completely of the record as a favor to The Governor. I am only here to speak for your hired henchmen as they are clones and do not speak much! Did you get all of that son?

[Dean] Yes, Sir! Uh. General. Look. I appreciate your candor but if your only here to talk for them then I'm pretty sure we really don't need you-

[Gov] Dean, relax dammit what's wrong with you?! General, please go on.

[General] *To The Dean* Do you understand what the term SQUAD LEADER WEAPONS EXPERT means?! WHEN PEOPLE CALL ME ITS BECAUSE THEY NEED ME SOMEWHERE, SO WHEN YOU PICKED UP YOUR PHONE AND SENT ME A MESSAGE YOU SAID YOU NEEDED ME SOMEWHERE, THAT SOMEHERE IS HERE, CORRECT?! Don't answer that I'm already over it. I'll be got damned if I let you give me another heart attack. Your henchmen son! Just because they're clones does NOT mean expendable! I said they weren't gonna talk to you that much they have families at home that they would like to get home to, remember your terms here kid steer away from casualties.

[Ellen] Sir I'd like to apologize for my brother he's a little primitive as of late he hasn't been interacting with people out in public.

[Dean] El, will you just. C'monnnn. He's a General he's not some sensitive little private. Sir. Please. Go on the plan , tell me how its gonna go.

Pan out as the General begins pointing at both people in the room and a monitor on the screen that is displaying blueprints and diagrams and maps. At one point The Dean also steps to the monitor and begins pointing at the screen as well while looking specifically at Ellen. Continue to pan out of room and out the building quickly up to the clouds.

June 6, 2027. Nevada State Bank located just off the Las Vegas Strip. Five years standing no attacks no threats. Security stands constant guard inside and outside the premises. The Post Commander on this shift is an old employee of the Dean's. He gives The Dean patrol patterns and other vital security information to be used by Ellen to shut down emergency alarms for three minutes after the hack. Timing is important. *Play Freddie Gibbs- The Hard*
Three large white SUV's pull up and park towards the back of the lot, it's not abnormal for rich people to come to the most accommodating bank in the most accommodating city. From the SUV's emerge six men. Two of the men run around towards the back of the building. Another two plant explosives at the doorway of the front entrance as they make way into the bank as regular patrons. The last two go to the trunk of one SUV and begin assembling three large assault weapons as they wait for their que. As all this happens The Dean gets out of one of the vehicles and behind him jumps out a beautiful dark-haired woman. The Squad

Leader. Rihanna, circa 2018... The Dean's Partner for this heist. The Governor comes through again. The Dean is handed an assault weapon and is lead to the entrance of the bank alongside his lovely partner by two now ski masked men also holding assault weapons. *BOOM* A large explosion blows the doors is and people can be heard screaming as the welcome party comes into the bank to greet everyone in attendance. Before bank goers can even get a chance again to breathe clean air after the explosion it's filled with gun smoke from the two weapons being rapidly fired for attention. One after another five bank security guards draw their weapons; almost simultaneous Three shots ring out. Seconds later, one after another, two security guards drop their weapons before they themselves drop to the ground. Dead! Immediately after that one of The Dean's hired guards falls to the ground as well. Dead! The two other remaining guards go over to the dead guards and retrieve their dropped weapons.

[Dean] *To himself* Fuck, I gotta pay for that. *Outloud* NOW THAT YOU ALL SEE HOW FAR MY REACH IS, I WANT YOU ALL TO PAY CLOSE ATTENTION TO ME! Allow me to introduce myself! I am the Dean of Crime; this is my lovely partner some of you may recognize her from being amazing since the year of 2010. Now that all the formalities are out the way if any of you want to see your children enjoy the future, I'll be guaranteeing them, I suggest you do as I say.
[Ellen]*in The Dean's Air Pod's* Alarms are cut Dean, you got 7 minutes, don't kill too many people.
[Random Man] I don't even fucking have kids! OH GOD!
[Dean] *Snaps*
[Random Man] *Is shot dead by Rihanna Circa 2018*
[Ellen]*In Air Pod* WHAT THE HELL?!
[Dean] This is not a funny story people, today will be tragedy stories for some, but for me. This is glory! And this is only the beginning! I will be the guiding force behind a new era of crime in America. The only reason I'm not killing more people is because all of you are going to go out and tell everyone you know that today marks the start of organized villainy in this country. *to skimask men* STUDENTS! Go check on your peers and help them finish up back there, reinforcements will be here soon and its almost lunch time!
[Ellen] *In Air Pods* 3 Minutes!
*students run to the back of the bank just as sirens can be heard approaching the area. The Dean of Crime demands all present bank staff stand and human barricade the front entrance, he then orders the bank visitors to sit in a large group immediately behind the human barricade. 2018 Rihanna collects everyone's wallets,

phones, bags, all belongings alike before she runs to the back as well. Almost simultaneously The Dean of Crime hears "Metro Police! Put the guns down and let the hostages go!!" and Ellen telling him time's up! He presses a detonator that triggers a large smoke screen at the doorway rendering the hostages invisible to the police department out front. The Dean of Crime empties his magazine into the ceiling as he runs to the back of the bank to join his students collecting money. Unaware of the situation, unable to see through the smoke screen, and ready to go on record as "fearing for their lives" the police engage fire after hearing all those gunshots as they breached the front entrance. Right through the human barricade consisting of the bank staff. Only the civilians sitting on the floor would live to make statements and tell stories. For the second time in his life The Dean was clearing five million dollars for having people killed. A successful heist. Minus 50k to the window of Mr. King the hired gun that passed during the heist. Media outlets throughout the country go insane while The Dean of Crime, his lovely new partner, and his students return to their secret campus to finish logistics and get everyone paid.*

*July 16, 2027 open in The Deans old office but now it has flowers and framed pictures on the desk, the chair is low and leather. Its raised up high and a grey fabric with pink accents. Candi walks in and sits down at the desk and sees an envelope, the same kind of envelope The Dean gave her the Christmas card in. She picks it up and opens it. Takes the card out to see a one-million-dollar check made out to The Organization. The children of this academy and academies across the nation will be educated because of this Futuristic Crime of Passion.

Gang Gang Girl Gang
Written By Marcus Colbert

January 23, 2026

      Good Evening, my stage name is Gal and I live in what is now only called New York where I work as a dancer at a popular gentlemen's club called Fat's Play Place. Except it's not a gentlemen's club, they just call it that. I started working at Fat's sixth months after my mother passed away which also happened to be my 17th birthday. Six months, it only took six months for my dad to fall victim to addiction and lose his job due to complications from the disease. Six months, it only took six months for my family to fall under the poverty line, six months until I had to take my first job as a drink girl at a dirty, low moral strip club. I worked there for a year or so on the nightly motivation that if I could work hard enough to keep my family afloat until my dad overcame his demons and saved me from this life then it might add some worth to the experience. All that motivation went out the window on a defining night six months before my 18th birthday, six months before my 18th birthday I was given my first promotion at Fat's, by Fat's himself, look at me climbing the corporate ladder. My new title was now "private dance girl" and my first project was to give a private dance to the birthday boy Mickey DeLano. You see, Mickey's dad was a very well connected legitimate business man supposedly untouchable, until about three months ago when him, his right hand man and about eight of his security guards were brutally murdered during the New York State New Year's Day Parade, so I was charged with the responsibility of keeping the fresh 21 year old new boss happy for the night. No one told me that part of keeping the kid happy meant being drugged and raped by him. Luckily for the girls with enough decency to help me I- "Gal!" A woman's voice calls from behind. "Gal there you are come on Allison found her man we got him in the alley behind the set. Come on he's fucking crying its hilarious!"

      I never got the chance to get any kind of justice or revenge for the intense trauma I was put through that night. I was never able to tell my dad before I lost him too. I kept the job and learned from my mistakes. I was never on the receiving end of that kind of treatment again. It wasn't long after that incident that I got together with four other girls and became what we now call Gang Gang Girl Gang. "Look Gal, I caught the son of a bitch! He picked up Trixie and took her right to the spot! He's fucking dead now. Ha ha ha!" Allison was our newest girl, it's been a long time coming for her, her initiation that is. She suffered through years of trauma at the hands of her gymnastics coach, but her parents insisted that she work with him if she ever wanted to make it to the Olympics. They refused to hear

a word of her many complaints and hints regarding the actions of her coach. Allison was my first true little homie, because she didn't come from Fat's like the rest of us. She came from a family of reasonably known Olympic athletes. Both her mother and father competed in the 2020 Summer Olympics which took place in Tokyo. Anyway! He was in the city for qualifying tournaments and being the ever-so-lovely scumbag, he is, Coach Heinrich Forther decided to stop and proposition the youngest (looking) girl he could find. That girl just so happened to be one of MY girls, long story short this asshole gets knocked out, tied up and brought to an alley behind an old warehouse that one of our girls inherited when a grandparent passed away. Coach Forther is about to find out just how every girl in this gang got full initiation. "Stacy go get the DoAs for Allison, it should be in the tub of lube" WAKE HIM UP AND TAKE THE BAG OFF! LET HIM KNOW WHERE HES AT AND WHO WE ARE! Allison rips the bag off his head and grabs his face for an eye to eye. The first words out his mouth was pretty much his last. He looks Allison in her face and says "G-Gwen, is that you? What is thi-" "THAT'S NOT MY NAME!!" Allison begins punching him in the face. He falls over in the chair he's tied to and nobody even makes a move to stop her as she continues to unleash years of pain on this man. Zoey doesn't step in until Allison picks up a lead pipe. She whispers something in Allison's ear and they both step to the side as Stacy walks up with a two footlong pole connected to the largest sex toy we could find. I can't remember exactly which girl was the first one to say, "dick on a stick" out loud but we all liked it and before we knew it, we adapted it and even pet named it "DoAs". GET THIS SCUMBAG OUT THE CHAIR AND BEND HIM OVER THE WORK TABLE! Stacy, Zoey, Crimson and Dez hold him the fuck down! Everyone else stand back and no looking away. ALLISON! Look at me! Are you ready? "Fuck this guy. He raped me. And then convinced my parents that I wasn't focused on training and suggested they take me out of school to train with him at his facility in the Midwest for six months with no supervision." There is no lesson to be learned here Allison. This is revenge. I hope its sweet baby girl. "I hope he can't relax!"
January 24, 2025

   "Good morning New York! This is Cal Rivers with the morning report. Another man found this morning reportedly raped to death in the lower westside of New York State, Agencies have started investigating but so far, no leads have been established. The Trial of Elon Musk continues! Where do you stand?! Do you believe he was brainwashed, or is the SpaceX tesla mogul going to be labeled as one of the evillest men to disgrace this Earth in the past decade? Find out more later in our day, but right now, were going to be talking to President Ocasio Cortez as she introduces new plans to rebuild more communities throughout the country. Stayed tuned into Morning News as we go through the following commercial break!"

Stacy and I are roommates. We have been ever since the night I was assaulted. When she noticed me lying unconscious in the private room, she immediately picked me up and carried me to the back. Stacy is 5'11, her stage name is Stacy, but her stage name is The Statue of Sexuality. When I came to, we had a brief but thorough conversation about what just happened, and she offered me her guest room just in case I didn't want to go home that night. I didn't want to go home. Since that first night and following morning Stacy and I have been best friends. She's the only girl at Fat's right now that has worked there longer than me. "We gotta go in like thirty minutes earlier than usual today okay? Fat's said he needs to talk to all of us. I hope we're getting raises or something Mario says he's getting the new Beamers down at his lot next month I want one." Bitch, If Fat's gives us all raises Ill pay the rent and bills for two months so you can get your Beamer. The only pay increase you can get is if you become his girlfriend and if you need the money that badly I'd suggest you go stroll before you lay up with that bastard. "Rockstar lifestyle might not make it! C'mon let's go I don't want to get stuck in traffic."

Stacy drives like a woman with money. Makes it really difficult to roll up and smoke weed in her car as she weaves in and out of traffic. She didn't always have such a wild streak, but I remember the night she flipped her switch though. In a way so did mine. We went out to upscale side of New York one night to celebrate Stacy passing her cosmetology exam finally becoming licensed. She worked so hard. It hurt all of my feelings when she told me that the guy who had just sent us drinks back in the bar was the guy who assaulted her when she was younger. That bastard sent us drinks, DRINKS! Then the smug son of a bitch had the waiter point him out at the bar so he could smile and wave at Stacy! I thought she was just ahead of the game until she dropped her drink and then ran out of the bar. I really didn't even get a chance to take a second look at him because I had to chase Stacy. When I caught up to Stacy she broke down and told me everything about her neighbor from down the street whom she had a crush on when she was younger. She also explained how that innocent crush turned into a traumatic experience during a school field trip. And that young man was sitting at the bar with a look that read as " I hope you enjoyed being assaulted, because I enjoyed assaulting you." We talked through last call and joined the leaving crowd. Stacy looked for her car and I looked for the smug bastard in a turtleneck. I found him before Stacy found her car and she still thanks me for it till this day. It was all a blur as we jumped him by his car drug him into the nearest alley, pulled his pants down, and violated him with an umbrella...

"GAL! Wake the fuck up faded ass! We're here bitch. Let's go hear what this fat fuck has to say." I hate this place so much. Every time I see the employee entrance, I think about burning this building down. Then I think about all the men and women who get drunk in here and accidentally or purposely drop all their money. The amount of men who pay for a "discounted private dance" and end up unconscious with their pockets turned out is amazing in my eyes. That statistic right there paid my rent six months upfront. Let's go hear what this fat fuck has to say.

"Listen girls, we're gonna have some rule changes around here." Fats says as he inhales hot wings. "Zoey, you're fired. Go see Banks and get cashed out before you go." Zoey slaps a wing out his hand and spits in the tray with the rest of the wings before storming out of the club. Fats pushes the tray to the side and cleans his fingertips before he goes on. "Crimson...Dez. You two are gonna be taking a pay cut. You'll be capping at 850 a night." Fats are you serious right now?! You just fire Zoey and let her walk out now you pull this shit on the twins?! Because what?! You have a gambling problem and no friends or family to try and stop you?! When you go too far into debt you cut our pay and take our jobs then string us back in when you can afford us. I swear I- "Gal! sshhshhshhshhh! What the fuck?!" Fats takes out a large wad of cash from his man bag and begins counting to himself as he talks. "Ya done Gal? Ya feel better now? Ya know it pains me to have let anyone go but times are hard and if ANYONE wants a job some people have to lose theirs. But even in the midst of all the devastation I still manage to have good news for you two. Crimson, Dez. The early birds will be showing up in an hour or so get everything ready make sure the drone bitches are in there getting ready for stage time!" Dez and Crimson give Stacy and I concerned looks before walking away. Fats sets down a large stack of money on the table before he addresses the two of us. "Look girls. I have a scheduling slash floor manager position I'm setting up but only one of you can take it, the other has to take this twenty-thousand-dollar severance and leave." Stacy and I briefly look at each other before I quickly reply I'll take the money! Stacy begins laughing and Fats handed me the money, gently pat me on the back and walked away. "Gal, I don't even know what to- Why?" I never wanted to do this Stacy, I just had to do it to feed my family. My dad passed away and my brother moved out of state when he turned eighteen, I'm done with this shit. You can have it. you were here before me anyway. You deserve this, it fits your persona better.

May 14, 2025

Knock Knock Knock "Gal open up! Stacy let me in before she left wake up, I need to talk to you!" Ugh! Hold on. Allison? Is that you? What are you doing on this side- okay, okay. I'm coming out. What's the problem?! "Gal it's- it's Forther! Well, not him but his people. They were at my house the other day when I went home to see my parents. It was random as fuck. Three big guys I don't know they looked pretty serious. They asked me questions. Like when did I talk to him last before he was murdered, if I know anything about what could have happened, I was kind of nervous but luckily it's been so long I just acted like I didn't remember anything." Allison what the fuck are you talking about?! What did you say to them?! YOU DIDN'T SAY ANYTHING DID YOU? This is the last fucking thing I need right now. "No. I know Stacy told me what happened at Fat's but I don't know I just said I haven't talked to him in years but they know I always tried to get him locked up for his misconduct with me as well as other girls in the program I was in." Okay, that doesn't sound too bad why are you so- *LOUD BANGING ON THE FRONT DOOR* Allison? What the fuck is- "Here, just take my phone password 1023 it has everything in it you'll need to help me. Just-" *BOOM* Three very large masked men break my door down and two of them grab Allison and drag her out my door. The largest of the three powers up to me and back-hands me down straight to the fucking ground. The last thing I see before black is Allison's phone bouncing across my floor and a pair of black metallic ridiculously Retro Jordan fives kicking shit over in my condo as they walked out. I'm going to fucking kill someone when I wake up.

   I wake up hours later still on my floor, all my shit still smashed and for three seconds that's the only thing I'm mad about. Then I remember what the fuck happened in the first place. I immediately get up and start looking around for Allison's phone. Fuck. My phone starts ringing. Stacy's calling on her lunch to check on me most likely. "Gal! Hello?! Are you watching the news?! Turn the tv and put on any news station!" why the fu- okay, give me a second what's the...rush... "Allison's parents are on the news saying she kidnapped by the Russian Mafia! Did she say anything when you guys talked earlier? Gal?? Are you there?! HELLO?! I'm coming home okay!?" I barely heard her last few words as I dropped my phone straight to the floor as I watched the news cover the story of my little homie being kidnapped most likely for a murder, I insisted she commit.

   "Good Evening New York this is Cal Rivers and if you're just now tuning in, we have breaking news from the Asani family that the youngest daughter, Gwen Asani, has been kidnapped. After receiving a ransom note and a follow up call, investigators are saying it may tie in with the family's association with Heinrich

Forther, an Olympic sports coach who was alleged to have former involvement with the Russian Mafia. "

I'm looking at all these pictures of... my Allison... their Gwen. As I listen to the story, I see how amazing she really is... was... is. I don't care. "Through many different generations we are all aware of the story of the Asani family. Owen and Gloria Asani both led men's and women's gymnastics teams to victories in the 2020 Olympic games which contributed to a very large overall win for America as at the time Americans were viewed as weak, unstable and irrational after Trump was elected for a second term. Her older sister took home multiple golds at the young age of 19 in the 2024 Olympics and Gwen was set to qualify for 2028 until she decided she wanted to give up all training and pull out of all obligations."

Stacy rushes into the house with Zoey, Crimson and Dez as I sit down on the couch. I'm fading in and out, but Stacy is saying something like "How did this fucking happen?! What the fuck happened to my condo?! GAL!" I immediately get up and get Allison's phone off the table where I left it when I got the call from Stacy. I put the passcode in and start looking through her stuff. Contacts list, photos, apps, notes, downloads. I don't know what I'm looking for, but I know something's there. LOOK! Allison came over here before she was kidnapped. She was kidnapped here! Three big fucking guys broke in, knocked me the fuck out— OWW! MY FUCKING FACE! MY HEAD IS POUNDING! They grabbed Allison and smashed all our shit before they left. Before they got here, Allison gave me her phone. She said it had everything I would need to help her in here. I don't know what she meant by that. I don't see anything that could be a clue in here. Dez takes the phone from me and begins scrolling through menu options. "she told you the pass-code right?" Yea. It's one zero two three. "Okay. I'm going to hook it up to my laptop and scan it for any info that was recently added. Maybe we can find something that stands out." Dez what the fuck you know about computer shit? "Yea remember I used to mess with that scammer guy, well part of scamming is computer and phone hacking, so here I am. A fucking nerd. Buuuut. Here's something that says it was added to her cloud files just an hour or so before you say she got here." We all look onto the screen as Dez pulls up a program that's pretty much a virtual map of the High Life Casino located in Las Vegas Nevada. "I mean this is crazy Gal, not only is this map super detailed room numbers on doors fire extinguishers and all that. It even has all secret paths and rooms included as well as a directory and guide." A fucking guide for what?! " I'm not sure okay?! Crimson, you wanna? I don't know how to read this shit." Crimson sits down and looks at the screen for all of five minutes before she starts talking. "It looks like some kind of legend that keys all the different colored lines used in the 3D map of the casino. So, like red lines indicated how the surveillance systems run throughout. Uhhhhhhm. Green lines lead from all hotel rooms to emergency exits. Blue lines are potential security patrol routes. It looks like there's one more line, but it has no description and it can barely be seen by the naked eye. I don't? you think I should invert it Dez?" I sit there in so much confusion as these two bottle girls, MY two bottle girls coding and running computer programs like they didn't run up a high five figure yearly shaking ass last year. In all fairness when we met the twins they had just graduated from an academy, but the education of our time was such bullshit we never really thought to ask if they had any other skills. I wanna ask who walks away from such a prestigious life to work but after everything that has occurred, it happens more often than I would've thought. "Okay bitch I got it! So, the 3D diagram you see here is under a specific filter. So, inverting does nothing, it's almost like that was TOO easy so she didn't do that, but Allison used our idea Crim. Which is almost just as easy but… only one of us would have known to try that." Crimson and Dez both look at each other. WHAT?! "Our senior year of high school Crimson and I created a program to track the movements of our school security unit using snapchat filters. Back then the program didn't work too well so we just left it alone. We told Allison about it one time and she thought it was funny but that's all until now I guess." Well, what the fuck happened now?! Why all the mysterious shit.

Crimson looks at all of us. "Because she used the same concept to make a plan for us to go save her. At least that's what it looks like. Black and white follows armed/unarmed guards guards, beauty filter follows housekeeping, there's a dramatic cool blue filter that I can only assume is our map because it breaks off into a heart aura filter that leads to a saferoom in the penthouse suite level and I'm sure this big ass "A" marks the spot where Allison is being held." Stacy grabs the laptop screen and shakes it. "So, what the hell Gal?! Allison wants us to save her?! You know this club is owned by dangerous fucking Russians, right? I-" Stacy! She's one of us. I don't care if she was rich and from a famous family, she was there for everything. She came from the other side of town one night and wound up being one of the most valuable assets to our group. She puts in work for the set and she's also kept ALL of us clean and professional on paper for the last year or so. So yes Stacy. We're going to save her. Or at least I'm going to. If y'all don't think one of our girls isn't worth it. Crimson and Dez look at each other and smile. "I mean, c'mon Stacy. This plan looks pretty good. It requires precision but with the right resources I think we can pull it. We gotta move fast though." Stacy, we need you girl. The plan only works if all five of us do our part. You're the only one of us with any combat training. You were in the military. "BITCH! I am a STRIPPER!

I mean, I'm not a stripper I work at a strip club, but I just got a promotion, so the title is, bitch you know you almost had the job. Ugh. Gal? for real? So what? We hit the casino floor in our best dick sucking dresses and flirt our ways into the penthouse suite?" Stacy will you at least listen to the plan. If Allison was smart enough to use a program the twins would recognize and be able to navigate, don't you think she'd have a specific place for all of us in the plan? Dez, I'm gonna put you in charge for the time being. Tell us what you got. "Okay. So. It looks like from top to bottom we're gonna have Crimson and I in the bottom floor level lounge hacking the system to cut cameras on que in the hallways that Stacy, Gal, and Zoey will be maneuvering through in order to infiltrate the penthouse suite and reach Allison. The camera cuts will only hold you through the first ten levels of the hotel but luckily enough the penthouse is on the twelfth level so at most I'd say you guys are looking at two maybe three levels of potential confrontations with these armed guards." Ugh. That is... that is pretty steep. I mean it's definitely dangerous, but I don't move around this city with a group of bad ass bitches for no reason. So were all fucking going to get her, and I don't want to say this for multiple reasons but. Or die trying. Look. Everyone go home and get some rest. Let me think on this and see what direction I wanna take on this.

May 18, 2025

I wait at home for the girls to get off work so we can put together the missing pieces to the plan Allison set up for us. I was glad to hear that Zoey was going back to Fat's. I mean, I hate that I was right about how he was gonna do us, but at least she's able to get that money again.

It's looking like we're gonna be taking a trip to a hotel casino in Vegas soon, so we all need money to walk with. Oh shit, they're talking about Allison on the news again! "Good Afternoon, this is Cal Rivers and if you're just now tuning in, we're here with the parents of young Gwen Asani, who has now been missing for going on 96 hours now. Her parents have remained strong through all the preceding investigations and have not given up hope as all leads turn up no results. They have received no contact since the original note that was left on their front door letting them know that their daughter had been kidnapped and nothing much else. Mister, Misses Asani, would you like to say anything to our many viewers and your many supporters? The floor is yours." I had never met, heard or even seen too many pictures of Allison's parents before all of this she really didn't talk too much about home life I can only imagine why, wealthy homes can be a little broken too. Hearing her mother talk about her, in almost the same voice as Allison's. "We don't know much about our daughter's outside life. I can't fathom why someone would want to do any harm to her she was such a sweet young girl. I don't want to say much right now but if Allison has any friends out there that may know anything. Please reach out to us through the news station we're willing to listen to any information that could help lead to Gwen's return. Thank you, Mr. Rivers." "Folks if you have any info that can help the Asani family in their time of need please call the tip line number you see at the bottom of your screen."

I turn the tv off and pick up Allison's phone. Search through her contacts list looking for "M". Mom. No. Mother. Weird. But that's Allison for ya. I copy the number into my phone and start a text, "I'm a good friend of Gwen's, except I know her as Allison. I want to meet with you." I press send and put my phone away as Stacy walks through the front door with all the girls behind her.

"Sup bitch you ready to go fuck up a casino this weekend?!" Stacy what?! The fuck is you talking about?! "Obviously we all thought about what you said last night! Duhhh! I mean. You kinda are the leader and we trust you. And also. We know Allison was special to you. She was special to all of us Gal. Dez went over the plan with me again and I think we can handle it if we stay down. We have no fire power but I'm sure if we put our money together I can talk to Mario and he-" Zoey suddenly speaks up "I know where we can get guns and smoke bombs and bullet proof vest and mad shit like that..." Zoey WHAT THE FUCK?! Okay. Where?! Let's hear it! "Well, you know my brother has always liked white women. Well, he married this white lady who's like super republican, not that it matters anymore, but anyway she's old school she has mad weapons and shit my brother lives on a big ass ranch and before I started rocking wit gang gang girl gang I'd go over there and shoot and blow shit up. She loves me for some reason. When my brother first told me about her I looked her up and uhhhh. She was not a big fan of black people back in the day. I mean... this is like five or six years ago." Bitch what the fuck we all niggas right here what you mean she wasn't a fan of black people five six years ago?! "She's. she's cool now, I guess. Can we just, ugh. Don't ask me anymore questions until you meet her. Come on, Ill drive us all out to my brother's ranch.

BITCH YOUR FUCKIN AUNT IS TOMI LAHREN?! What the fuuuuuuuuu. I kind of just fade off as Tomi bounces up to all of us surprisingly not aging as bad as you'd expect a white woman to age, maybe she is cool now? She grabs Zoey and gives her a big hug, Zoey hugs back. NOW I have questions! Tomi says to Zoey. "Sup BITCH! Long time no see I miss you girl! Who are they? Who ya'll running from? Haha I'm Kidding! Nice to meet yall! I'm Tomi, some of yall may know me from being a racist bitch on tv, I'm not sure yall look pretty young. Twitter maybe? ANYWAY! What brings you up my way girl, ya know your brother's not here right? You ain't talk to him before he went on tour?" "Aunty Tomi, this is Gal, Stacy Dez and Crimson. These are my bitches, for life. We have a problem and told them you might be able to help us." Well what's up baby? Talk to me. Come on! Let's go to my office. Why are we standing around when I got a full bar and a pound of mhmmmm waiting for me in there?!" I'm not really growing on Tomi's offscreen persona, but I trust Zoey enough to let her help us if she really is this cool. She takes us into her office and the walls are teeming with untold political secrets. Maybe this won't be as bad an experience as I'm thinking. I might pick up on game if I'm being honest with myself. Tomi's a bitch, but she's low key a self-made bitch, I can respect that.

"Y'all go ahead and make yourselves some drinks while someone tells me what it is exactly that you need from me." I look over at Zoey and she looks back at me and nods for me to start talking. Look, Ms. Lahren. Or ya know. Tomi. One of our friends was kidnapped and is currently being held by the Russian Mafia at the High Life Casino in Vegas. She's our newest and youngest member and if she hadn't been running around with us this might have never- "Hold up bitch, did you say Russian Mafia?! Mhmmm. So yall gone need guns then huh? Those block face fuckers are dangerous. Everyone carries in those casinos. Come on. We need to be in the war room. The fuck are we drinking and smoking like yall just needed money or something." All five of us finish our little drinks and Dez grabs the blunt as we hurriedly follow Aunty Tomi to the "War Room". "Look I don't have time to itemize I got shit to do. Zoey baby take war bags three and four please be careful. If you need anything else, please just call me."

May 19, 2025

I don't remember how I got home last night, and I still have a killer headache from getting knocked out. I know we went out to celebrate and laugh at Zoey for being all buddy-buddy with "Aunty Tomi". I know everyone pretty much slept here though; I can remember that much. I also know that both war bags are just sitting in the middle of the living room because we all agreed that we were too messed up to be playing around with live weapons. I walk out into the living to find Dez at the table on her laptop and Crimson is cleaning my kitchen. Lovely. I love my bitches.

Where's Stacy and Zoey? "They are currently at like a Target or Walmart right now buying all of us everything we need to pack and make it to our flight to Vegas on time." Both Dez and Crimson go about their business like Dez didn't just say all five of us are getting on a plane and going to Las Vegas, Nevada. LAS. VEGAS. NEVADA. ON THE WEST COAST! WHAT THE FUCK DO YOU MEAN PACKED TO MAKE IT TO OUR FLIGHT TO VEGAS ON TIME?! So casually? Crimson stops cleaning and walks over to me. "Gal calm the fuck down. We all knew that once Tomi gave us all that shit the next step was to actually go out there and make a move to get Allison back. We had a long fucking night and you've had a long fucking week. Sit down girl. Check your phone." Well. When she puts it like that, I have no choice but to listen to her. I sit down. Look at my phone and begin going through messages and morning shit. Crimson goes on. "Ya know. No one else would say anything, ya know cuhz we all know how strong you are. But Imma say something cause that's me ya know? We've been worried about you. All of us. You've been here with us all this leading us, but it's a little like you got kidnapped along with Allison. I'm ready to get the bastards that did this to her, you, us." Looking through my messages I have the usual stuff I skip past or barely reply to. One random number message saying, "She dies May 23." Dez what the fuck is this?! Can you like trace a number for me? "I already have the number; we all got the message early this morning. Almost right after we all got back here and fell asleep. I looked it up and it's a Wi-Fi only number associated with the same IP address used in some of the coding within the program that Allison had in her phone for us." So, pretty much? "Yes. Allison found a way to tell us, whether she already knew or if she's just finding out now, we know."

This is so much to take in. Can we do this. Can I do this. I haven't been on a plane since I graduated high school and went to visit my brother in California. Wait. How are we gonna get on a plane with all that military shit?! CRIMSON HOW THE HELL ARE WE GONNA GET ON A PLANE WITH- before I get a chance to finish my sentence Stacy and Zoey bust through the front door carrying at least ten bags each including a couple suitcases. My bitches so useful and resourceful. The two drop all the bags and Dez moves them over to the table. Stacy looks at me and smiles. "OKAY! So! We got literally everything you need for a vacation slash assault on a mob in a casino and I honestly think we might be able to leave some shit. I didn't know what we'd be wearing so we kind of just got a little bit of it all you never know. We got plane tickets for you, Crimson and Dez. First class no lay overs you're welcome bitch. I called Mario to tell him I was going to Vegas for business and that fuck said he was taking a private jet out there with his boys for someone's birthday! Fucker wasn't even gonna tell me! HA! I convinced him to let Zoey and I ride along with the "war bags" if we partied with them during the ride. He invited other girls that bastard so it's whatever."

Stacy what the fu- you're amazing girl. But, before we uhh. Lock into this next action scene we got coming up. I just wanna let you know that I have absolutely no idea what's waiting for us in that casino. There's a reason we're going in with guns. I want everyone to just follow the plan to the closest detail as possible. We already lost Allison I don't want to lose anyone else to this lifestyle. We have to protect each other the best we can. We can't afford to make any mistakes because we have no idea if these Russians are leaving us with even the slightest margin of error. Even if they are, I'm sure they'll be working hard to stitch it up. When do we all leave Stacy?

May 22, 2025 Location: Las Vegas, Nevada

The twins and I arrived at the hotel Stacy set us up to stay at by midafternoon, or what I assume is midafternoon since it was bright out, the streets were already crowded and I fell asleep on the plane so I had no idea what was going on. Luckily enough Crimson and Dez were slightly experienced travelers so they got us through check in with no problem. We get to our room and not even a minute of us being inside we get a knock on the door. Open it up and Stacy tells us to come over to her room next door, that's the war room complete with multiple computer monitors all featuring camera angles within the High Life hotel. Bullet proof vest and all kinds of weapons lay on tables and the beds. It's tomorrow or never now…

May 23, 2025

I barely got any sleep last night. I couldn't stop thinking about Allison. The idea of her being a couple thousand yards away from me. That text message in my phone. I came all this way and if I can't at least take a few lives trying to save hers, then I would be incomplete forever. Or dead.

The twins arrive at the High Life Casino/Hotel at 6AM and go to the 24-hour café. From their combined laptops the two of them should be able to cause two separate power outages in the building: the first is going to breach security systems and allow Stacy, Zoey and I to gain entrance with all our gear at the service level. From there we follow the maps on the app that Allison left for us. Disguised as house keeping the three of us draw no attention while we make our way through casino floor and hotel level. We weren't scheduled to run into any confrontations besides a few people asking for towels and shit. Stacy leads us to the last service elevator lobby that leads to the penthouse level, where only exclusive members and Russian mob fucks have clearance to be. That's also where this program created by Allison has led us all to believe she's being held at. Zoey pushes our service cart to the side, and we change into our gear and get ready for the live action levels. At this point the twins are scheduled to meet us in this lobby as well because we need full force to breach the entrance and gain any kind of momentum. They're a little late. It's no problem, until a tall Russian fuck walks past the lobby and looks in towards us. Before he even notices our weapons out, I notice this blonde hair prick is wearing the same kind of shoes as the guy who kicked my ass and trashed my condo. So, I charge him and with all my body weight I tackle his ass into the wall. I don't even get a chance to tell Stacy why we're jumping this guy, but I guess she just knew because she jumped in with me immediately and Zoey just loaded up the bags and started pushing elevator buttons. We had already put him to sleep by the times the twins got there but it was a good fight. I'm gonna go trash his shit now. We hid his earpiece in the bottom of a plant before we hopped in an elevator and made our way up to the Penthouse level. Stacy looks at me, "Was that a bad guy or were you just trying to get us all hyped about this next scene?" I straight face back her for a second then I laugh. That was the mother fucker that knocked me out and trashed our shit when they uhhh... kidnapped Allison. But that wasn't the guy that grabbed her. I just recognized his shoes. In this moment I feel a weird sense of relief that you normally wouldn't feel while you're taking an elevator ride up to what could possibly be your last moments alive. The girls break out in laughter for a second and then the elevator comes to a smooth stop.

Everything pauses for a second before the door opens. We all pile out and navigate via the map for two levels through the stairs before meet a big freaking Russian mob guy at the doorway going out onto the third floor. He put a pretty good fight. I don't think Zoey has ever been hit like that before, but unfortunately Stacy had to shoot him for putting his hands on one our bitches. Club rules. No touching the girls. Sorry for your luck player. BUT NOT BEFORE THIS BASTARD PULLS THE DAMN FIRE ALARM NOW WE GOTTA HURRY THROUGH THIS SHIT WITH A HIGHER CHANCE OF GETTING SHOT AT! THEY JUST CUT OUR MARGIN OF ERROR TO AN EVEN THINNER SLICE, DEZ DROP A SMOKE BOMB AND CUT THROUGH ROOM 419 WITH US! THE MAPS UPDATE WITH SHORTCUTS IN THE CASE THAT AN EMERGENCY ALARM IS TRIGGERED THIS BITCH ALLISON IS A GENIUS! Okay. Sshh. Shh. Quiet now. Look. We can stay in here until all the guards on this level get over here and start checking through the rooms. Dez, Crimson. You guys still have one power override left in your hack system, right? Crimson shows me her phone screen, "Yes. We can use it to override the interior power and kill all the lights once the guards give signal to scan through the rooms." Ah! Bitch! Get out of my head that's the idea! Okay. Gear up while we wait for the guards to show up. They see that dead guy out there trust me they're going to get as many hands as possible on this one. The smoke screen will make them paranoid but the moment they feel secure enough in numbers to spread out I want you to dead all the lights and everyone go night vision. We need to take out as many of these bastards as possible because more are going to come but we need to keep the ratio even as we maneuver through these last couple levels to get to the room, we think Allison is being held in.

It doesn't take more than five minutes for what looks like 100 guards to fill this big ass hallway. I look over to the twins and signal them to cut the power. As soon they do, we kick the door out to the hallway to cut and shoot through each and every guard on that floor. The only way to the final level is an elevator, one way n one way out and with multiple alarms, dead guards on different floors, and two oower outages in one day it was pretty safe to say they were waiting for us. We all stand off to the side when the door finally whizzes open and Zoey tosses out a smoke bomb. Nothing. By now we should hear the faint sound of smoke pouring out of the device at the very least, but no. Zoey peaks around the corner. "It's gone." What the fuck do you mean it's gone? Suddenly the backwall of the elevator starts moving, it's either gonna push us out into the hallway or close use into the front walls. We rush out into the hallway and take cover in the first entryway that can shield us all. That's when they start shooting back. At least three of them, at least 90 shots.

I signal for Crimson and Dez to cross the hallway to another entryway while Stacy covers them, Stacy is the best shot. They take the bait and Stacy wings one of them when the twins cross the way and draw them out. Stacy hangs out to long and gets grazed. Stacy's tough. She's not too worried about it. The twins air the hallway next and catch two more guards trying to cross the way. I swear between the five of us we had all angles covered but none of us noticed the elevator door had opened again. We didn't notice the two guards walk out either, until it was too late. I turned around and shot one as he shot Dez two times and the second scattered at Stacy, Zoey, and I. He grazed me and hit Zoey in her shoulder. Aunty Tomi didn't raise no punk though. She clipped him down

The three of us cover each other and move over to another entry way further up the hallway. We manage to take out another three guards on our way, but the real kick is that guards are still slowly but surely coming into the hallway from both angles. Our world continues to crumble slightly as we look back to see Crimson holding up her barely alive twin and still shooting guards. I turn back and cover her to signal for her to move when its clear. "Bitch if you think I'm leaving my dying sister Ill fucking kill you myself! I'm gonna smoke the elevator and carry Dez over to one of these rooms and try to hide out and cover you! You guys go ahead!" I can't take any more time screaming down this hallway, but I can't leave her, them here. "Allison knows! Just go! I'll be fine I promise!" She throws the smoke bomb into the elevator and carries her sister into one of the rooms. Strong ass bitch.

Zoey sets a charge to the door and we all get ready to kick it in. the app says that Allison is on the other side of this door. The lock blows and Stacy creeps in first, and I follow her. Zoey backs us up and as soon as she passes through the frame the door whizzes shut and Stacy and Zoey are hit with Tasers. Someone knocks me in the head with something and then a cloth bag is put over my head. I'm fading in and out but I know I was sat down and tied to a chair. I can hear muffled screaming, but I don't know who it is. Last, I remember Zoey and Stacy were being dragged away by guards. I hear a voice say "Lemme see the bitch's face" and someone snatches the bag of my head. I look over to one side of the room and see Allison tied to a chair as well. Gagged. Bleeding. But still alive. Across from me sits a mean looking guy in a really nice suit. He has pictures on his desk of him and some guy I kind of recognize but can't wholly put my mind on it at the moment. He speaks to me. He has a really scary voice. "That's my brother. Nice guy. Well at least a lot nicer than me. The Dean. You know. From what Allison tells me. You kind of remind me of him but let me tell you this: the only reason you're not FUCKING DEAD RIGHT NOW IS BECAUSE YOU WORK FOR ME NOW. Don't forget that. Allow me to introduce myself. I'M THE GOVENOR AND I OWN YOU BITCH.